Hey Diddle Diddle

Retold by Brian Moses
Illustrated by Jill Newton

Jill Newton

"I live by the sea in Somerset with my dog, Bob, and my horse, Spinney. I spend my time running, riding and drawing."

Hey diddle diddle,
the cat and the fiddle,

The cow jumped over the moon.

The little dog laughed
to see such fun,

And the dish ran away with the spoon!

Hey Diddle Diddle

Hey diddle diddle,
the cat and the fiddle,
The cow jumped over the moon.
The little dog laughed
to see such fun,
And the dish ran away
with the spoon!

Can you point to the
rhyming words?

Hey Diddle Doodle

by Brian Moses
Illustrated by Jill Newton

Brian Moses

"I have a golden labrador called Honey who spends a lot of her time trying to get through the garden fence to visit the poodle next door."

Hey diddle doodle,
the pipe and the poodle,

The frog hopped over the star.

The big tiger roared
to see such tricks,

And the fork zoomed away in his car!

Hey Diddle Doodle

Hey diddle doodle,

the pipe and the poodle,

The frog hopped over the star.

The big tiger roared

to see such tricks,

And the fork zoomed

away in his car!

Can you point to the rhyming words?

Puzzle Time!

How many cats and dogs can you see in this picture?

Answers

There are 4 dogs,
and 6 cats.